NATASHA WING'S
The Night Before
Class Picture Day

To all you photographers who make us look good—NW

To the one and only Shutter Speed Kid . . . with love—AW

No part of this publication may be reproduced, stored in a retrieval system, or transmitted in any form or by any means, electronic, mechanical, photocopying, recording, or otherwise, without written permission of the publisher. For information regarding permission, write to Grosset & Dunlap, an imprint of Penguin Young Readers Group, a division of Penguin Random House LLC, 375 Hudson Street, New York, NY 10014.

ISBN 978-1-338-18884-4

12 11 10 9 8 7 6 5 4 3 2 1   17 18 19 20 21 22

Printed in the U.S.A.   40

First Scholastic printing, March 2017

NATASHA WING'S

The Night Before
Class Picture Day

By Natasha Wing
Illustrated by Amy Wummer

SCHOLASTIC INC.

'Twas the night before picture day
and in homes everywhere,
all the parents were fretting
over unruly hair.

Children with straight locks
soon would have curls.

Boys' bangs were trimmed up,
and so were the girls'.

Then they practiced in front
of their mirrors for a while,

until they perfected
a most flattering smile.

Outfits were picked out
and hung up with care.
Shirts were rejected
if they had one teensy tear.

The children then nestled
all snug in their beds,
while visions of cameras
flashed in their heads.

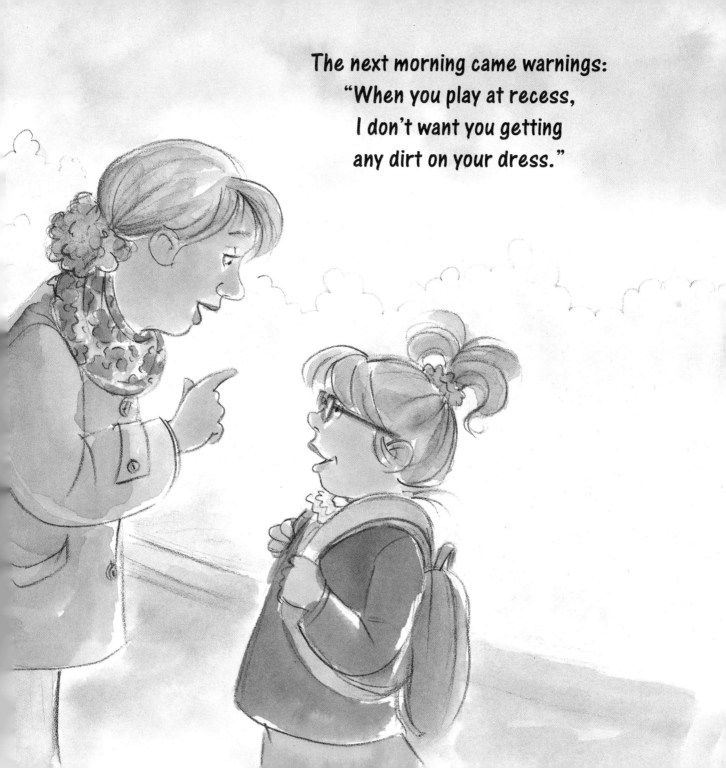

The next morning came warnings:
"When you play at recess,
I don't want you getting
any dirt on your dress."

"Remember to smile!" parents called,
still making a fuss.
"We will," kids chimed back
as they climbed on the bus.

Everyone stayed clean—
they truly did their best . . .

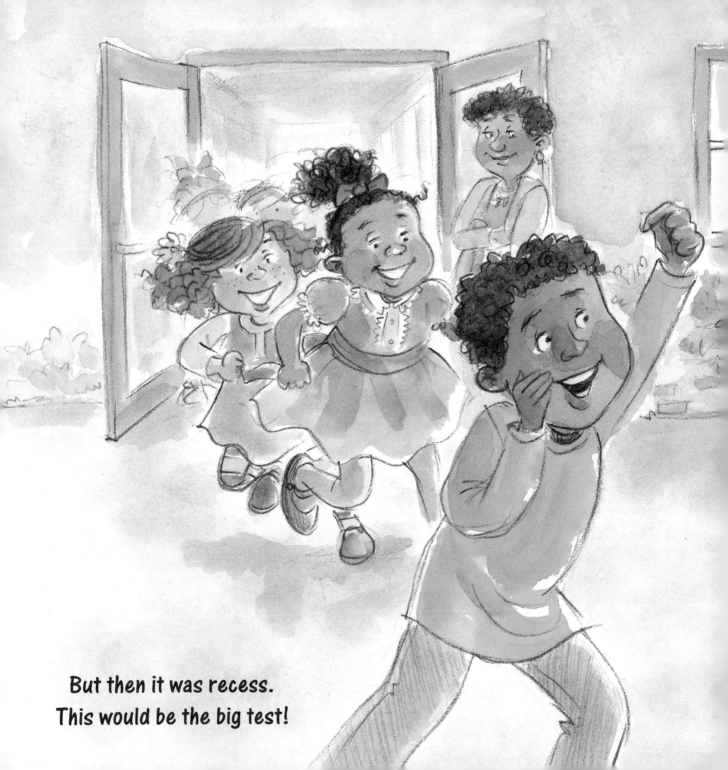

But then it was recess.
This would be the big test!

In a great game of dodgeball,
things got a touch out of hand.
Not everyone stayed tidy
as their parents had planned.

José lost a tooth,
and Rob tore his shirt.
Lizzy lost her bow,
and Kim stained her skirt.

But that didn't stop
the photographer that day.
With a "Look here and smile!"
she—*flash*—clicked away!

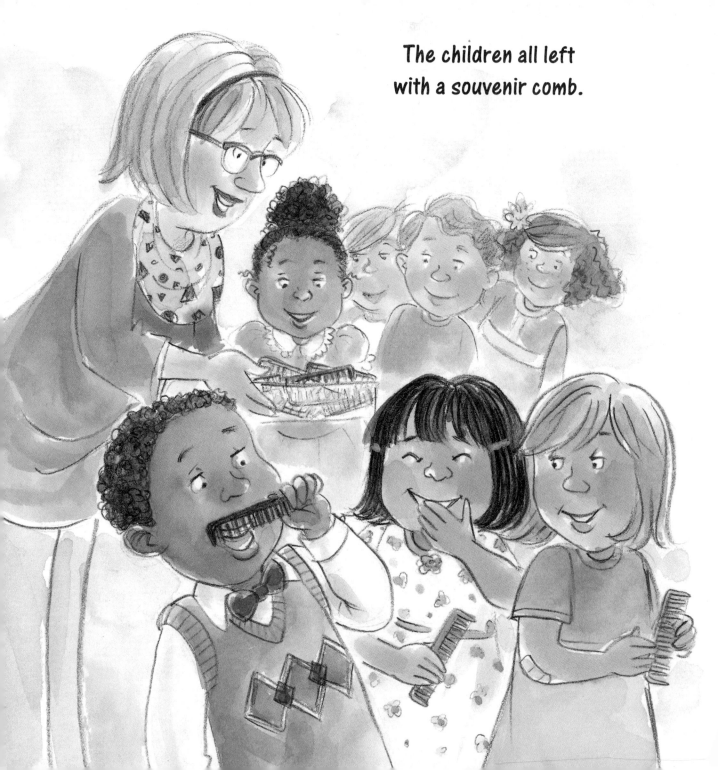

The children all left
with a souvenir comb.

A week later came pictures
of themselves to take home.

When what to their parents' eyes should appear
but a packet of photos of their little dear.

Their smiles—oh so smiley!
Their teeth—pearly white!

"Oh no! What's that?"
some moms said with fright.

There was jam on someone's glasses,
and blue paint on someone's nose.

Most eyes were wide open,
but a few were tightly closed.

Still, most families were happy—
their photos turned out okay.
For the others, thank goodness,
there's a do-over day!